A NOTE TO PARENTS

When your children are ready to "step into reading," giving them the right books is as crucial as giving them the right food to eat. **Step into Reading Books** present exciting stories and information reinforced with lively, colorful illustrations that make learning to read fun, satisfying, and worthwhile. They are priced so that acquiring an entire library of them is affordable. And they are beginning readers with a difference—they're written on five levels.

Early Step into Reading Books are designed for brand-new readers, with large type and only one or two lines of very simple text per page. **Step 1 Books** feature the same easy-to-read type as the **Early Step into Reading Books**, but with more words per page. **Step 2 Books** are both longer and slightly more difficult, while **Step 3 Books** introduce readers to paragraphs and fully developed plot lines. **Step 4 Books** offer exciting nonfiction for the increasingly independent reader.

Library of Congress Catalog Card Number: 97-67476
ISBN: 0-679-88706-7 (trade) — ISBN: 0-679-98706-1 (lib. bdg.)

Printed in the United States of America   10 9 8 7 6 5 4 3 2 1
STEP INTO READING is a registered trademark of Random House, Inc.

 A BIG TUNA TRADING COMPANY, LLC/J. R. SANSEVERE BOOK

Step into Reading®

MERCER MAYER'S
CRITTERS OF THE NIGHT®
MIDNIGHT SNACK

Written by
Erica Farber and J. R. Sansevere

A Step 1 Book

Random House New York

Wanda Jack Thistle Bones Axel Seer Snake

Capt. Short Bob Dracul Duck Wolf Mouse

Groad   **Frankengator**   **Moose Mummy**

Uncle Mole   **Zombie Mombie**   **Auntie Bell**

It is midnight.

Twelve o'clock.

Let's go, Groad.

Time to rock.

Knock! Knock! Knock!

Guess who's there?

Meanie Greenie.

Hello, there!

Come right in.

Have a seat.

Ready, set,

time to eat!

Toe of frog.

Eye of newt.

And, of course,

a piece of fruit.

Knock! Knock! Knock!

Who could it be?

Stinky Pinky.

Come and see.

Do not,

do not,

do those things!

Slugs on toast,

topped with cheese.

The magic word?

Just say *please*!

Mellow Yellow.

Take a bow.

French-fried ants.

Cream of goo.

Close your mouth

when you chew!

Clear your plates.

Wash your spoons.

The sun will rise

very soon.

Scrub the walls.

Clean the floor.

Sweep the dust

out the door.

Good night, Groad.

Monsters, too.

Good night, kitchen.

Good night to you!

Groad does not
make a peep.
You know why?
He's fast asleep!